Gum

in a H

Val Biro

CW00841129

CLAREMONT
BOOKS

Published by the Penguin Group
Penguin Books Ltd, 27 Wrights Lane, London
W8 5TZ, England
Penguin Books Australia Ltd, Ringwood,
Victoria, Australia
Penguin Books Canada Ltd, 10 Alcorn Avenue,
Toronto, Ontario, Canada M4V 3B2
Penguin Books (NZ) Ltd, 182-190 Wairau Road,
Auckland 10, New Zealand

Penguin Books Ltd, Registered Offices:
Harmondsworth, Middlesex, England

This edition first published in Great Britain in 1983
by Hodder and Stoughton

This edition published by Claremont Books,
an imprint of Godfrey Cave Associates Limited,
42 Bloomsbury Street, London, WC1B 3QJ,
under licence from Val Biro, 1996

Copyright © 1983 Val Biro

Printed in Italy   All rights reserved

ISBN 1 854 71789 8

One fine day Mr Oldcastle set out for a quiet drive in Gumdrop.

'Mr Oldcastle! Mr Oldcastle!' came a cry. It was his fat neighbour, Mr Bumblebee.

'We must catch the 4 o'clock train and we can't find a taxi. Please take us to the station!'

This won't be a quiet drive after all, thought Mr Oldcastle.

So out came the Bumblebee family. Mr B. tied their luggage to Gumdrop's rack, the family piled in, the engine started first time, and they were off.

'Hurry! Hurry!' cried Mrs Bumblebee, because it was already half past three.

Soon she cried out again. 'Stop! Stop! I forgot to turn off the gas!'

So Mrs B. clambered out and waddled all the way back to her house. 'Hurry! Hurry!' she cried as she came panting back again.

Gumdrop went as fast as he could. But there were potholes in the road and he bounced so much that all the luggage fell off!

'Stop! Stop!' cried Mr Bumblebee. So they jumped out to collect their scattered cases. Mr Oldcastle tied them on the rack again. 'Hurry! Hurry!' wailed Mrs B.

Gumdrop went as fast as he could until they came to the main road. There they were soon stuck in a traffic-jam.
'Hurry! Hurry!' squealed Mrs B. as she stood up to shoo the cars away with her umbrella.

'We shall take a short-cut,' said Mr Oldcastle and he turned left. But the road at the far end was closed. So they had to turn left, and then left again. And they were back in the traffic-jam. Only much further back!

'We shall take that street on the right this time,' said Mr Oldcastle. 'It is an even better short-cut.'

'Hurry! Hurry!' shrieked Mrs Bumblebee, waving her umbrella. 'It is ten to four already!'

The street was empty and Gumdrop
went as fast as he could.
'We shall make it yet!' said Mr Oldcastle,
glancing at Gumdrop's clock. But the
thermometer said BOILING. And a big
cloud of steam shot up from the radiator.
'Stop! Stop!' shouted Mr Bumblebee.

Gumdrop had run out of water. So the children fetched some from a nearby farmhouse. By the time they returned with a jugful, it was five to four.

'Hurry! Hurry!' cried Mrs Bumblebee in despair.

Gumdrop went as fast as he could,
skidding this way and that. Mrs B. kept
her umbrella in front of her face. It was all
too much for her.
'Hurry! Hurry!' she whimpered.
'There's the station at last!' cried Mr
Oldcastle. It was one minute to four.

The Bumblebees scrambled out,
grabbed their cases and raced helter-
skelter to the platform.
But there was no train. Only a notice
which said:

THE
4 O'CLOCK
TRAIN IS
DELAYED.
IT WILL LEAVE
AT 4.30

'Well,' said Mr Oldcastle, mopping his brow. 'I told you we would make it. What's more, there is time for a cup of tea!'

'Oh, thank goodness for that,' said Mrs Bumblebee who suddenly felt much better.